MW00934233

with very best wishes,

Daniel Walter

# THAT FAT CAT
## WHO CHANGED HIS WAYS

**DANIEL WALTEN**

Illustrated by JO-ANNE BUTTON

BROWN BOOKS KIDS

© 2022 Daniel Walten

All rights reserved. No part of this book may be used or reproduced in any manner without written permission except in the case of brief quotations embodied in critical articles or reviews.

This is a work of fiction. Any similarity to real persons, living or dead, is coincidental and not intended by the author.

*That Fat Cat Who Changed His Ways*

Brown Books Kids
Dallas / New York
www.BrownBooksKids.com
(972) 381-0009

A New Era in Publishing®

Publisher's Cataloging-In-Publication Data

Names: Walten, Daniel, author. | Button, Jo-Anne, illustrator.
Title: That fat cat who changed his ways / Daniel Walten ; illustrated by Jo-Anne Button.
Description: Dallas ; New York : Brown Books Kids, [2022] | Audience: Ages 4-8. | Summary:
That Fat Cat is, well, fat. He can't even see his toes anymore. He loves food and sleeping too much! He eats biscuits and pies, sausage and peas. He simply gorges on milk and cheese. All that eating makes him sleepy, so much so that he can't even do his only job, to chase away the mice. The other household pets know something must be done! While That Fat Cat naps, the mice take away all the food in the house. Butch the Dog, a retired champion racing greyhound, takes it upon himself to train That Fat Cat to live a healthier lifestyle. That Fat Cat must change his ways!--Publisher.
Identifiers: ISBN 9781612545677 | LCCN: 2021922517
Subjects: LCSH: Cats--Juvenile fiction. | Dogs--Juvenile fiction. | Mice--Fiction. | Obesity--Juvenile fiction. | Weight loss--Juvenile fiction. | Nutrition--Juvenile fiction. | Physical fitness--Juvenile fiction. | Health--Juvenile fiction. | CYAC: Cats--Fiction. | Dogs--Fiction. | Mice--Fiction. | Obesity--Fiction. | Weight loss--Fiction. | Nutrition--Fiction. | Physical fitness--Fiction. | Health--Fiction. | BISAC: JUVENILE FICTION / Animals / Cats. | JUVENILE FICTION / Health & Daily Living / General.
Classification: LCC: PZ7.1.W3596 T43 2022 | DDC: [E]--dc23

ISBN 978-1-61254-567-7
LCCN 2021922517

Printed in China
10 9 8 7 6 5 4 3 2 1

For more information or to contact the author, please go to
www.BrownBooksKids.com.

## DEDICATION

This book is dedicated to the most discerning, open-minded,
imaginative, and precious audience of all . . . our children.
To all the children and grandchildren in my life, I've loved
every minute of watching you grow . . . it's been a blast!

## ACKNOWLEDGMENTS

As a young actor starting out at the world-renowned Chichester Festival
Theatre in England, I had the great experience, at the request of artistic
director Patrick Garland, of performing in children's theatre. It was there I
learned to appreciate what a wonderful audience children are. Make no
mistake, they are a tough crowd and can be devastatingly critical if you don't
meet their expectations, but get it right, inspire their boundless imaginations,
and the rewards are immense. To ignite the imagination of a child is to grasp
the tail of a comet—it's a wild ride and rewarding beyond measure.

That Fat Cat really loved to eat,
he ate so much couldn't see his feet!
He laid around upon his back
and fancy that, That Cat got fat!

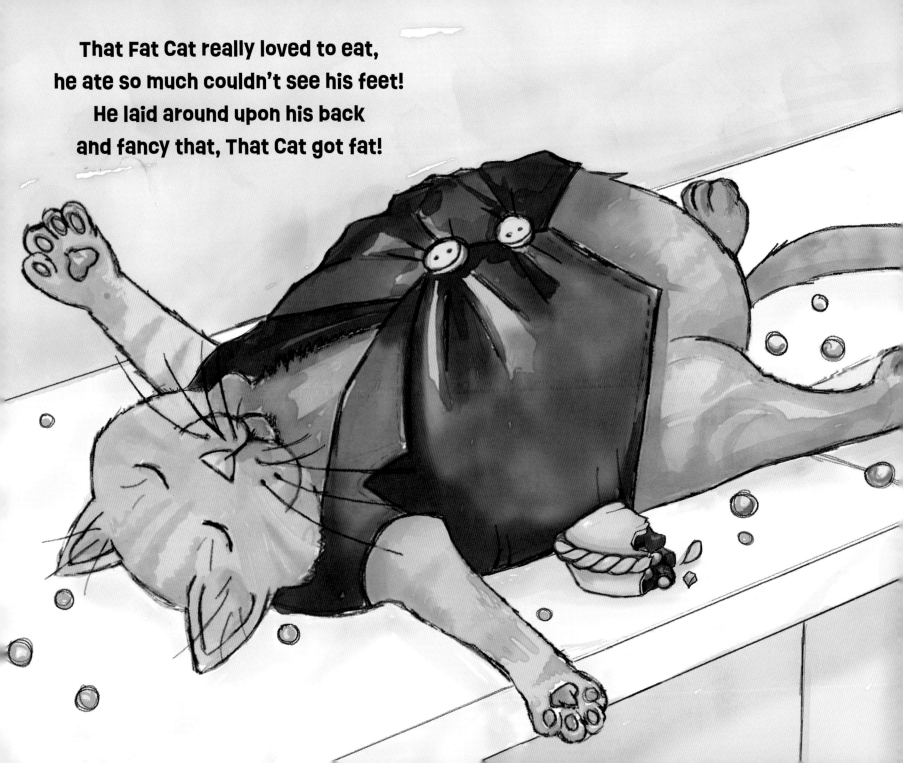

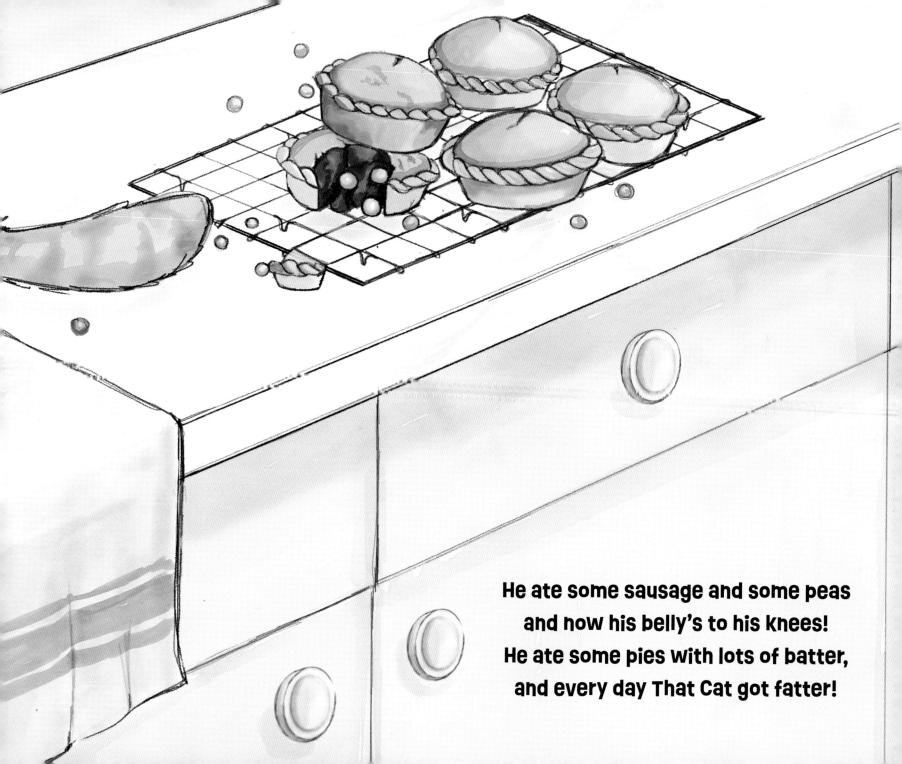

He ate some sausage and some peas
and now his belly's to his knees!
He ate some pies with lots of batter,
and every day That Cat got fatter!

He ate some cakes

with lots of cream,

then closed his eyes

so he could dream

of sweets and cookies and for sure

he dreamt of eating even more.

He drank his milk, ate lots of cheese,
and mice could do just as they pleased.

They walked around without a care,

all knowing they were safer there . . .

. . . than any other place they'd choose

as Fat Cat took another snooze!

They could lay out across his paws
and even fiddle with his jaws!

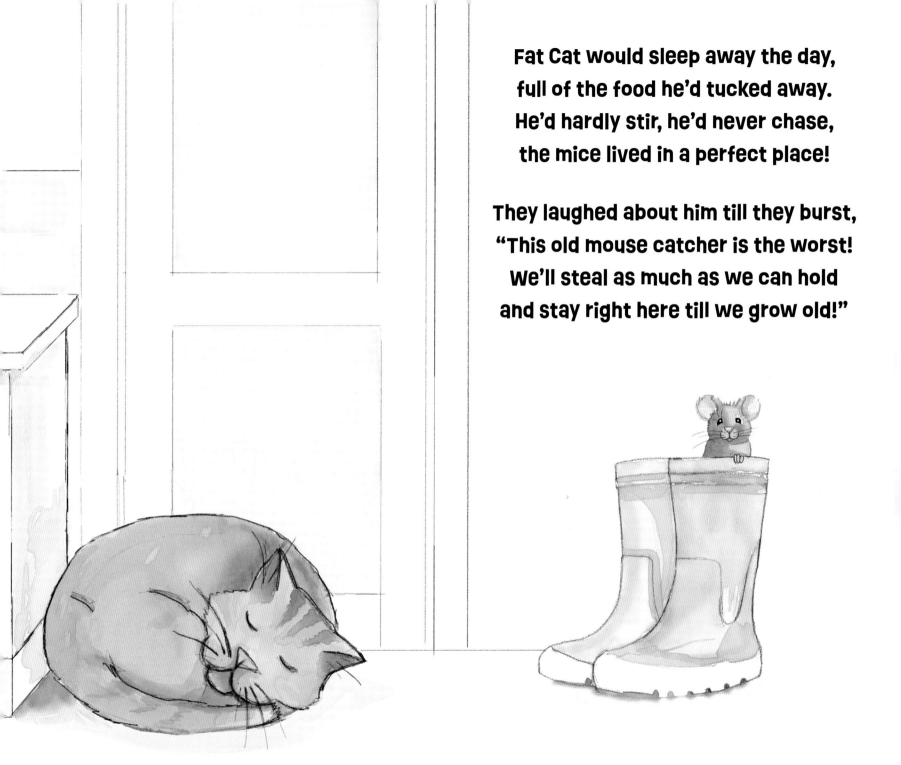

Fat Cat would sleep away the day,
full of the food he'd tucked away.
He'd hardly stir, he'd never chase,
the mice lived in a perfect place!

They laughed about him till they burst,
"This old mouse catcher is the worst!
We'll steal as much as we can hold
and stay right here till we grow old!"

The neighbor pets were getting cross,
"This old Fat Cat is such a loss!
The mice can run and steal and rob
because That Cat won't do his job!"

They held a meeting in the park,
they talked and talked till it was dark!
"This is a mess to solve together
or the house will be lost forever!"

"It's known," they said, "to me and you,
chasing mice is what they do!
That Fat Old Cat is just too slow,
he has to change or has to go!"

Butch the Dog cannot be quiet,
"That Fat Cat must change his diet!
It seems to me it can't be plainer . . .
I must be That Fat Cat's trainer!"

An athlete Butch was born to be,
champion racer clear to see,
and even though he is retired,
he had the knowledge they required.

The pets went to their meeting place
so they could all talk face to face.
"We're so concerned, concerned indeed!
To do your job, you must have speed!"

"Bad food and drink will make you tired
and lose the fitness that's required.
It's important that you know,
we say this as we love you so!"

That Fat Cat knew his friends were right
so studied hard both day and night.

He learned that all you eat and do
makes you happy and healthy, too!

Healthy Diet

So Butch the Dog
devised a plan,
the Fat Cat jumped
and stretched and ran!

He turned about,
he chased his tail,
and Butch made sure
he did not fail!

He was in charge
as Fat Cat trained,
walking even
when it rained!

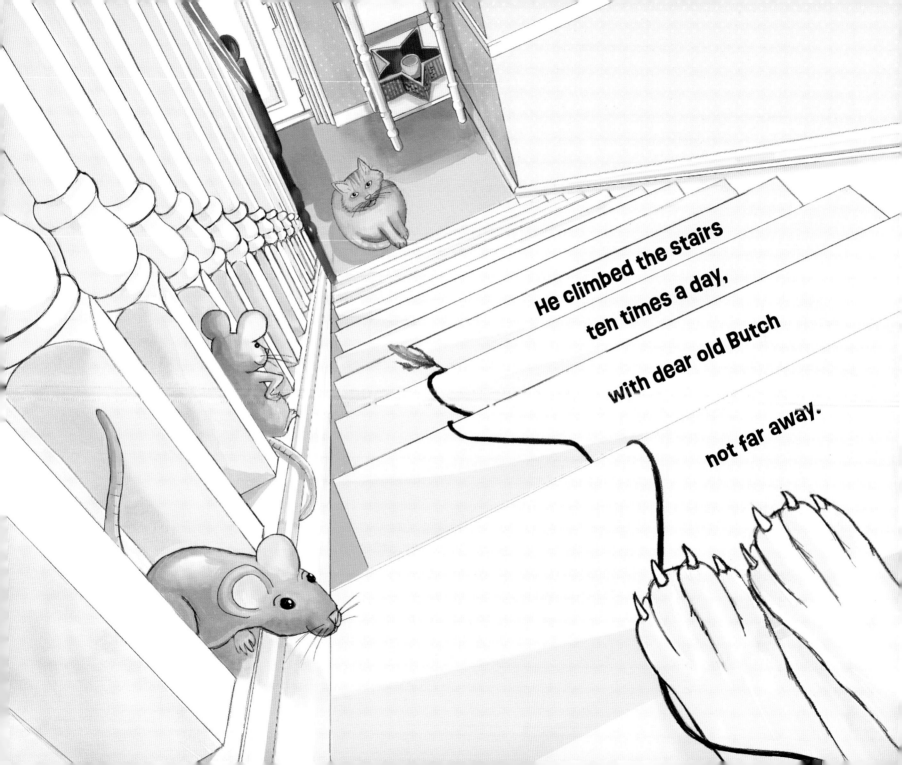

He climbed the stairs
ten times a day,

with dear old Butch

not far away.

He put in place a diet plan,
to teach Fat Cat all he can
about the need to always choose
a way to eat he'll never lose.

He ate his fish with lots of green,
to make him fit, to make him lean.
He munched his meat to make him strong
and trained with passion all day long!

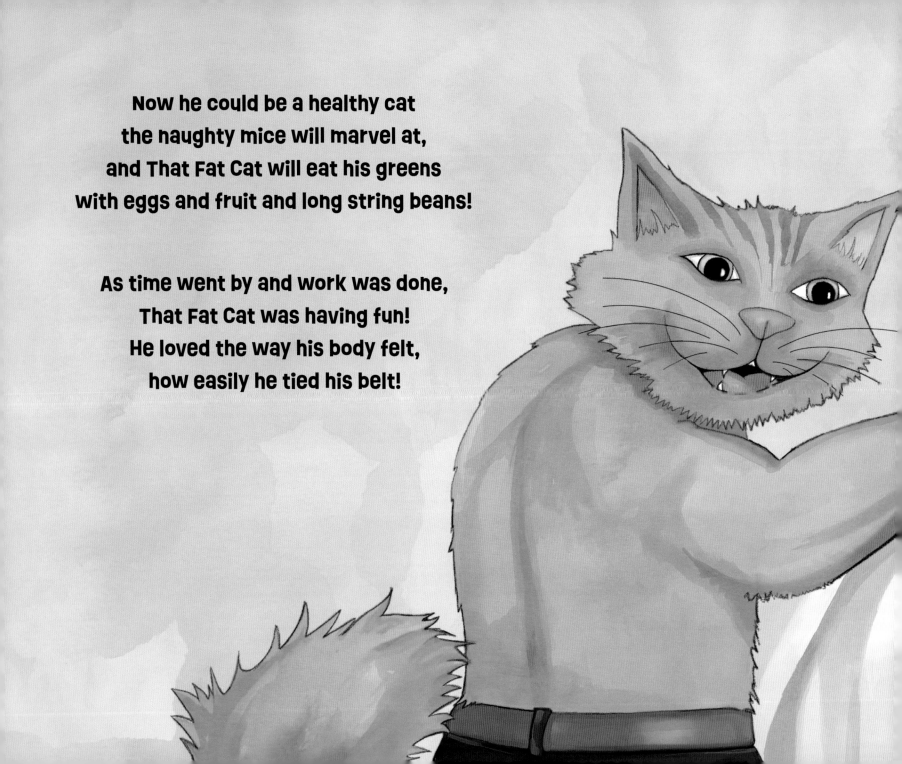

Now he could be a healthy cat
the naughty mice will marvel at,
and That Fat Cat will eat his greens
with eggs and fruit and long string beans!

As time went by and work was done,
That Fat Cat was having fun!
He loved the way his body felt,
how easily he tied his belt!

Butch the trainer was very pleased
how That Fat Cat could see his knees.
His big fat belly disappeared,
and all his pet friends cheered and cheered!

So Fat Cat learned cakes are just treats,
and special days are for the sweets.
Smaller portions, nothing bigger
would keep him such a handsome figure!

Then a whole new cat appeared,
a cat that those mice truly feared,

for he could run as fast as they
and soon he chased them all away!

They packed their bags, they left their hole
and left behind the cheese they stole,
and That Fat Cat was fat no more,
he stood so tall and prowled the floor . . .

More focused than he'd ever been
to be a catching mice machine,
That Fat Cat had changed his ways
and stayed that way . . . for all his days!

## ABOUT THE AUTHOR

Daniel Walten is a British author, actor, and singer. He divides his home life between London, England and the United States. Born in Hampshire, England, he spent his early childhood in Singapore and began traveling and performing at an early age. He enjoyed a long and successful career in British theater and television and now tours the world as a solo performer and writer. His hugely popular "Made in England" show is a regular fixture in Las Vegas, high-end cruise ships, and venues in the US and UK. He is a regular performer for Top Rank promotions at World Championship boxing events featured worldwide on ESPN, BT Sports, and Fox Sports, performing the British national anthem for several world champions including Britain's Tyson Fury and Amir Khan. In this enviable position, he has enjoyed some of the greatest highlights of his career and has performed many times at Madison Square Garden in New York, MGM Grand Las Vegas, AT&T Stadium in Dallas, The Forum in Los Angeles, and T-Mobile Arena in Las Vegas, among others.

## ABOUT THE ILLUSTRATOR

Jo-Anne Button, known as Jo to her friends, was born and brought up in England. From an early age she was never without a pen in her hand, and at the tender age of six she aspired to be a designer and illustrator. She graduated with a bachelor's degree in graphic design from the Norwich School of Art and Design. For the past twenty years she has worked in the advertising and publishing industry and has illustrated for magazines.

Jo is married with a daughter and two rescue cats that provide continued inspiration for her drawings, both of which are featured in the book.